HOW TO DR...

STEP-BY-STEP

#BEST SELLER BOOK

POKÉMON

THIS BOOK BELONGS TO

DRAW CUTE UMBREON

1.

2.

3.

4.

5.

6.

7.

8.

9.

10.

11.

12.

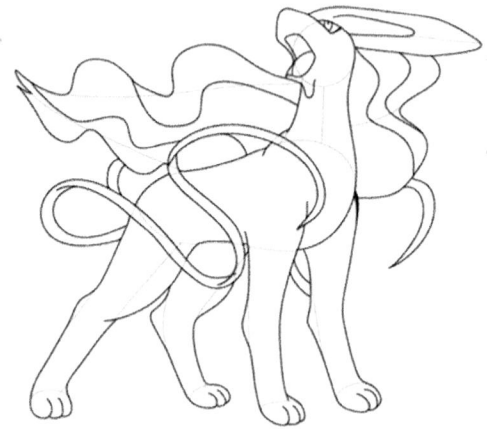

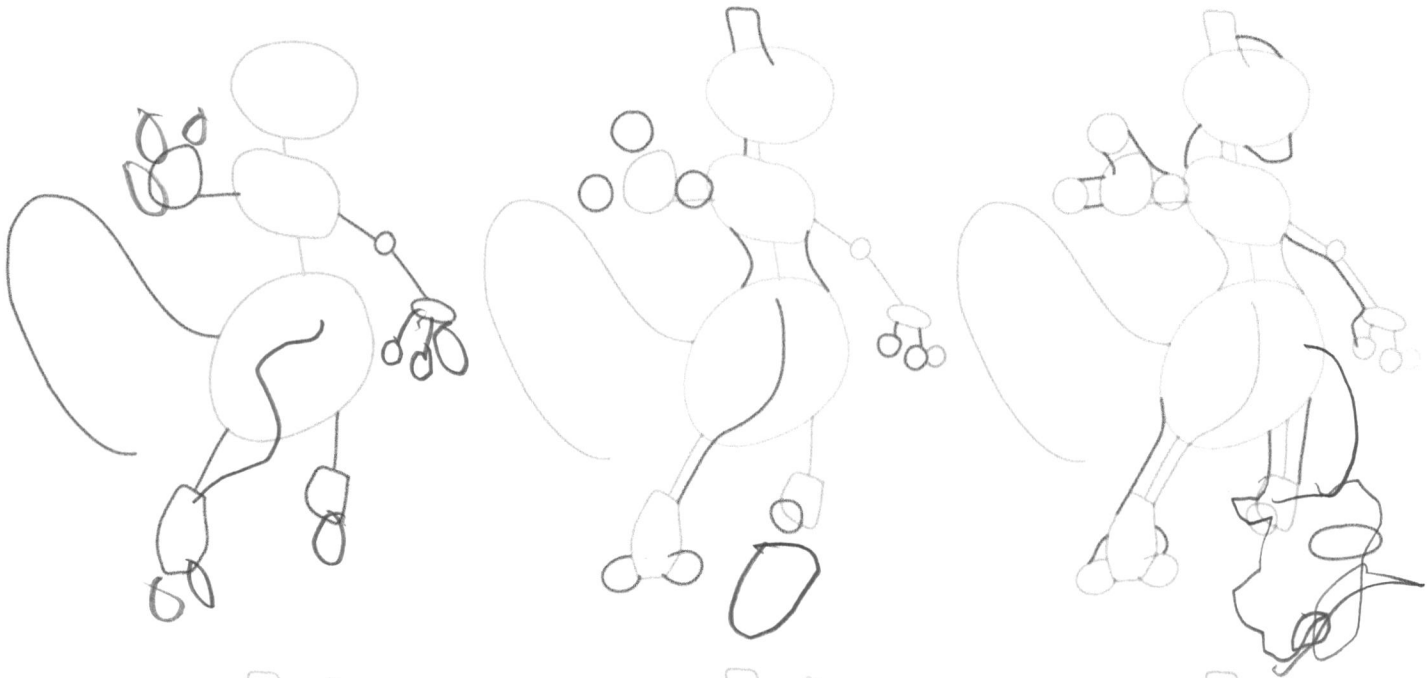

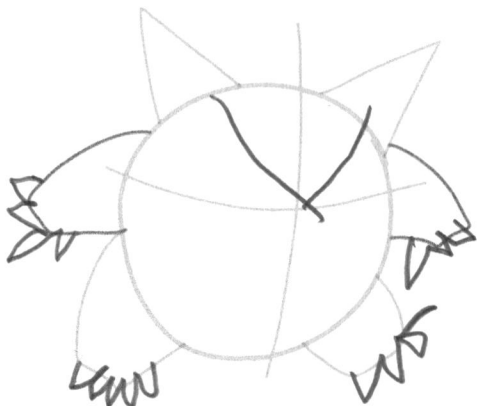

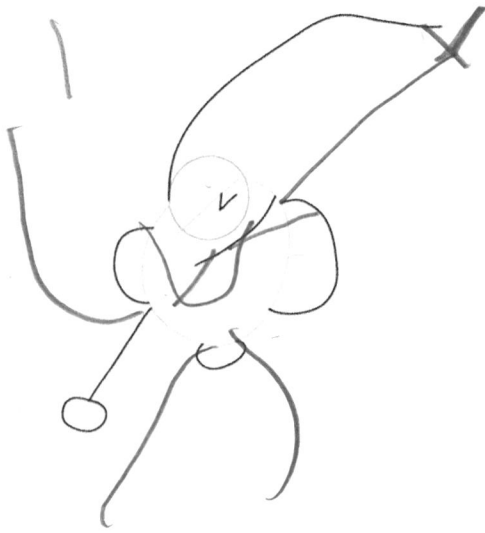

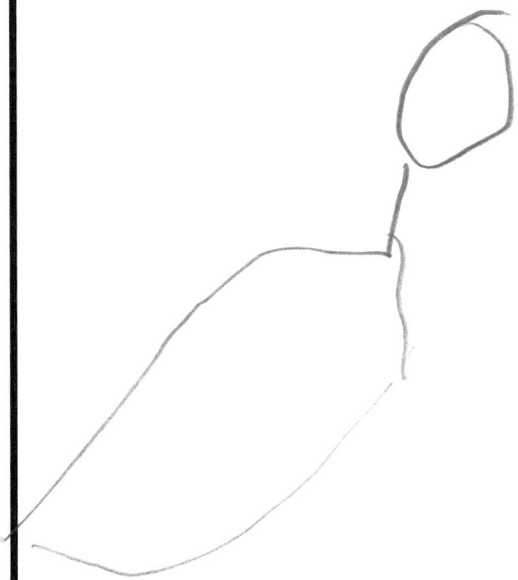

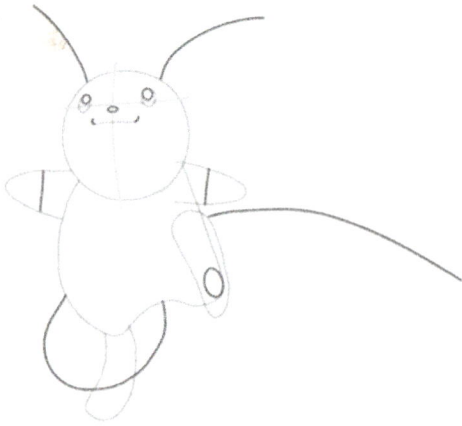

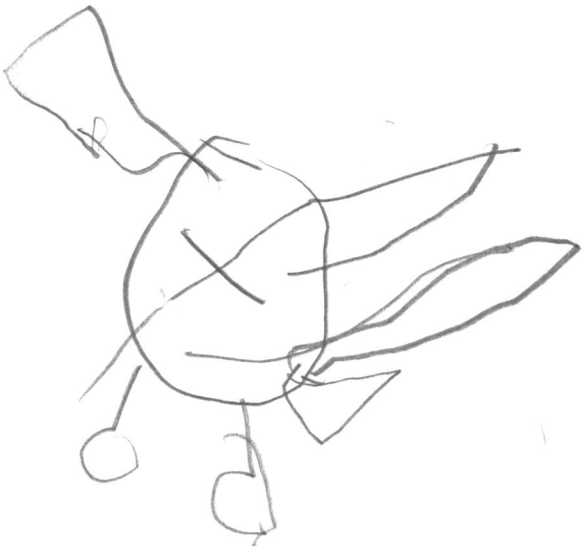

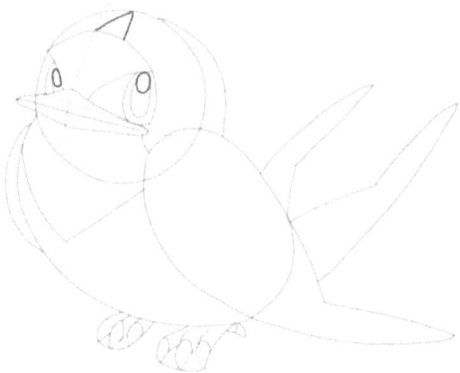

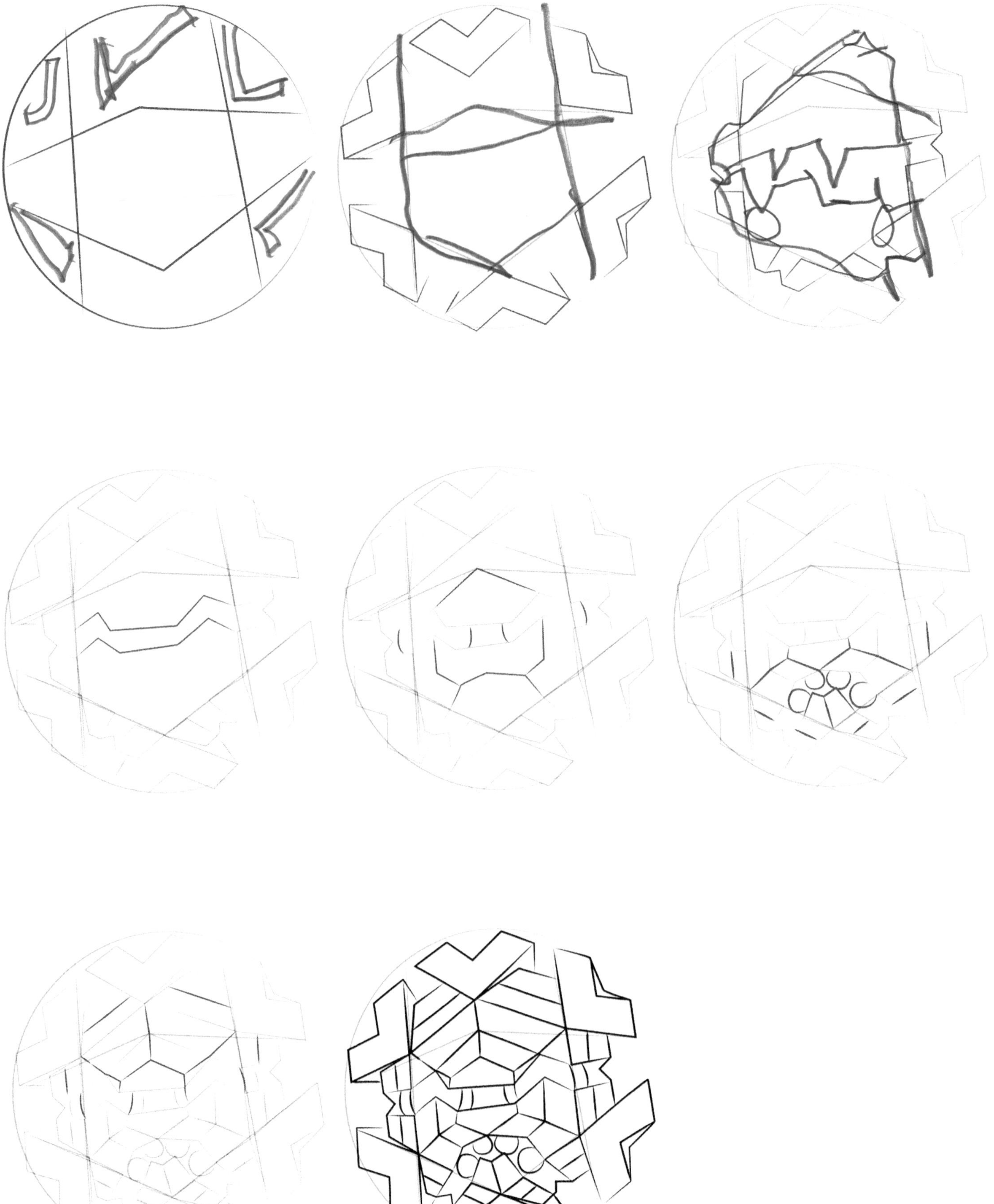

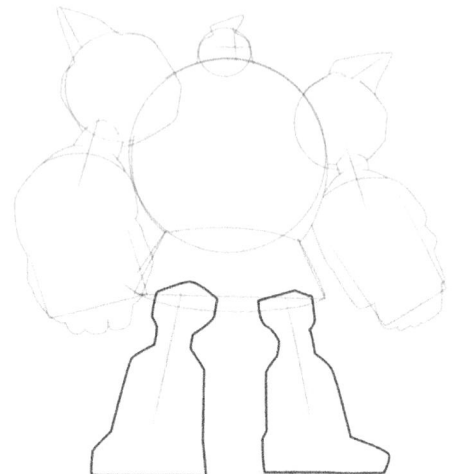

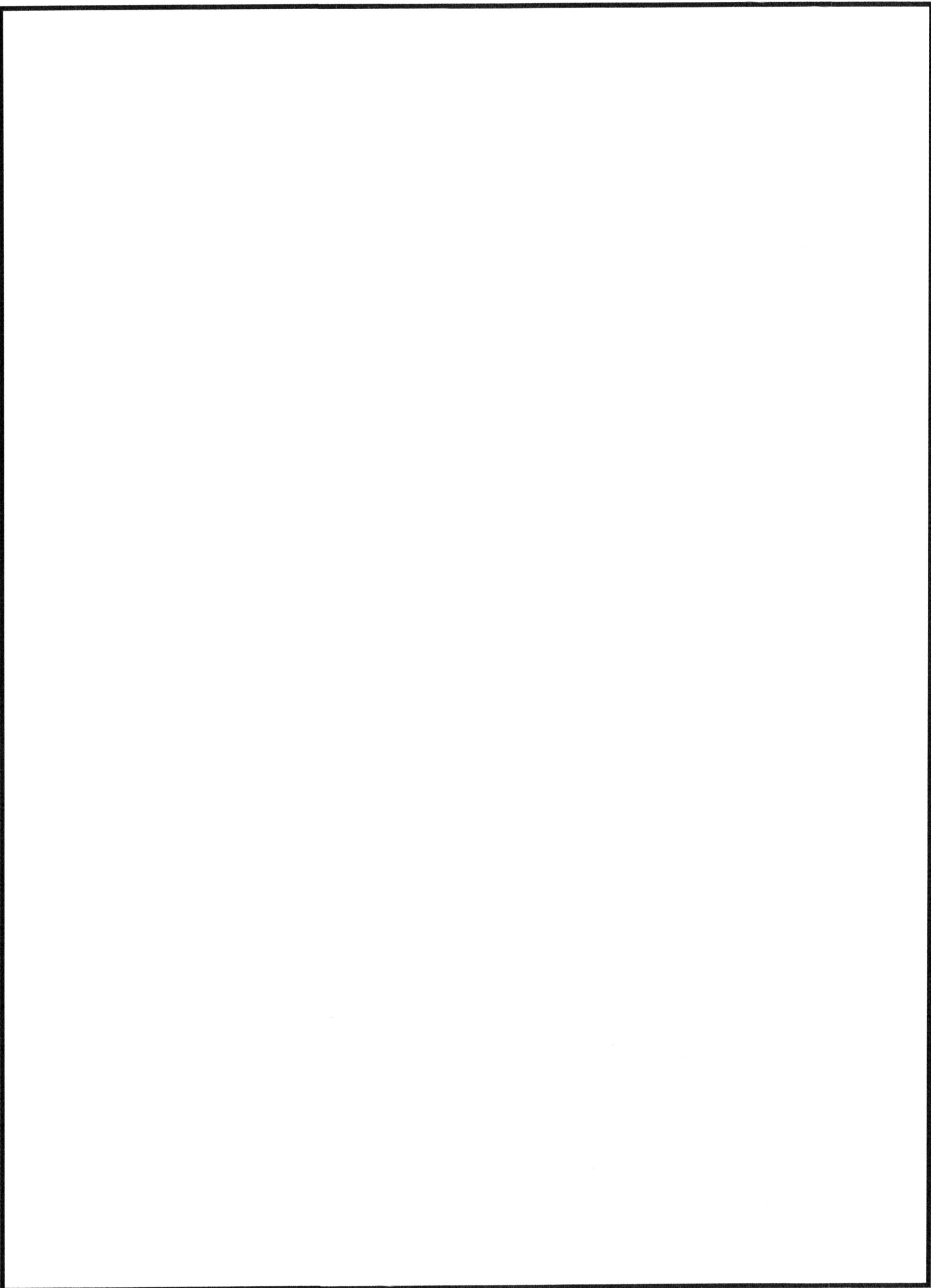

Printed in Great Britain
by Amazon

84648904R00066